Mrs Pepperpot's Christmas

Story *by* ALF PRØYSEN

Illustrated by BJÖRN BERG

Translated by MARIANNE HELWEG

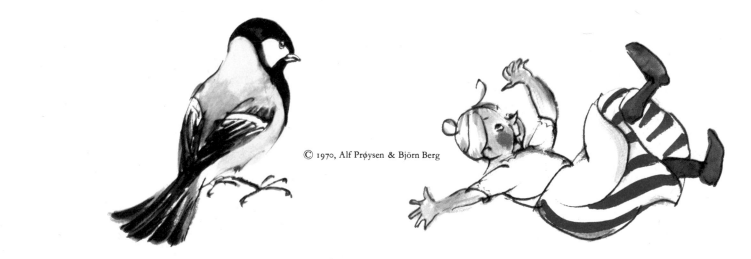

PUFFIN BOOKS

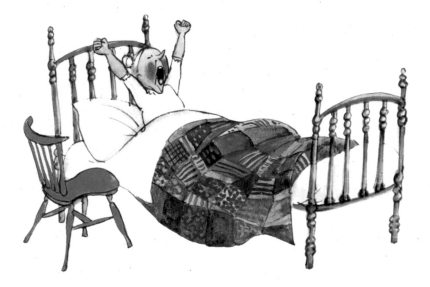

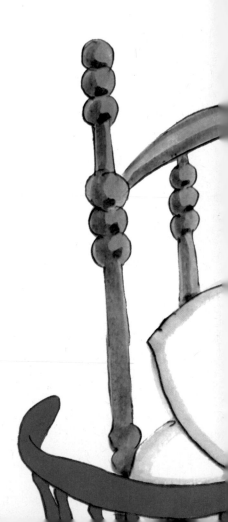

There was once a little old woman who went to bed at night like everyone else, but sometimes in the morning she would wake up and find that she had *shrunk* to the size of a pepperpot. As it happens her name was Mrs Pepperpot.

This was one of those mornings, and Mrs Pepperpot climbed to the top of the bed-post and swung her legs while she wondered what to do.

'What a nuisance!' she said. 'Just when I wanted to go to the Christmas Market with Mr Pepperpot!'

She wanted to buy a sheaf of corn for the birds' Christmas dinner, and she wanted to get them a little bird-house where she could feed them every day. The other thing she wanted was a wreath of mistletoe to hang over the door, so that she could wish Mr Pepperpot a 'Happy Christmas' with a kiss. But Mr Pepperpot thought this was a silly idea.

'Quite unnecessary!' he said.

But Mrs Pepperpot was very clever at getting her own way; so even though she was now no bigger than a mouse, she soon worked out a plan. She heard her husband put his knapsack down on the floor in the kitchen and—quick as a flash—she slid down the bed-post, scuttled over the doorstep and climbed into one of the knapsack pockets. Can you see her?

Mr Pepperpot put the knapsack on his back and set off through the snow on his kick-sledge, while Mrs Pepperpot peeped out from the pocket.

'Look at all those nice cottages!' she said to herself. 'I bet every one of them has a sheaf of corn and a little house for the birds. *And* they'll have mistletoe over the door as well, no doubt. But you wait till I get home; I'll show them!'

At the market there were crowds of people, both big and small; everyone was doing their Christmas shopping, and there was plenty to choose from! At one stall stood a farmer selling beautiful golden sheaves of corn. As her husband walked past the stall Mrs Pepperpot climbed out from the knapsack pocket and disappeared inside the biggest sheaf of all.

'Hullo, Mr Pepperpot,' said the farmer, 'how about some corn for the birds this Christmas?'

'Too dear!' answered Mr Pepperpot gruffly.

'Oh no, it's not!' squeaked the little voice of Mrs Pepperpot. 'If you don't buy this sheaf of corn I'll tell everyone you're married to the woman who *shrinks*!'

Now Mr Pepperpot hated people to know about his wife turning small, so when he saw her waving to him from the biggest sheaf he said to the farmer: 'I've changed my mind; I'll have that one, please!'

But the farmer told him he would have to wait in the queue.

Only a little girl saw Mrs Pepperpot slip out of the corn and dash into a bird-house on Mr Andersen's stall. He was a carpenter and made all his bird-houses look just like real little houses with doors and windows for the birds to fly in and out. Of course Mrs Pepperpot chose the prettiest house; it even had curtains in the windows and from behind these she watched her husband buy the very best sheaf of corn and stuff it in his knapsack.

He thought his wife was safe inside and was just about to get on his kick-sledge and head for home, when he heard a little voice calling him from the next stall.

'Hullo, Husband!' squeaked Mrs Pepperpot, 'Haven't you forgotten something? You were going to buy me a bird-house!'

Mr Pepperpot hurried over to the stall. He pointed to the house with the curtains and said: 'I want to buy that one, please!'

Mr Andersen was busy with his customers. 'You'll have to take your turn,' he said.

So once more poor Mr Pepperpot had to stand patiently in a queue. He hoped that no one else would buy the house with his wife inside.

But she *wasn't* inside; she had run out of the back door, and now she was on her way to the next stall.

Here there was a pretty young lady selling holly and mistletoe. Mrs Pepperpot had to climb up the post to reach the nicest wreath, and there she stayed hidden.

Soon Mr Pepperpot came by, carrying both the sheaf of corn and the little bird-house. The young lady gave him a dazzling smile and said:

'Oh, Mr Pepperpot, wouldn't you like to buy a wreath of mistletoe for your wife?'

'No thanks,' said Mr Pepperpot, 'I'm in a hurry.'

'Swing high! Swing low!
I'm in the mistletoe!'

sang Mrs Pepperpot from her lofty perch.

When Mr Pepperpot caught sight of her his mouth fell open: 'Oh dear!' he groaned, 'This is too bad!'

With a shaking hand he paid the young lady the right money and lifted the wreath down himself, taking care that Mrs Pepperpot didn't slip out of his fingers. *This* time there would be no escape; he would take his wife straight home, whether she liked it or not.

But just as he was leaving, the young lady said: 'Oh Sir, you're our one hundredth customer, so you get a free balloon!' and she handed him a red balloon.

Before anyone could say 'Jack Robinson' Mrs Pepperpot had grabbed the string and, while Mr Pepperpot was struggling with his purse, gloves and parcels, his tiny wife was soaring up into the sky.

Up she went over the market-place, and soon she was fluttering over the trees of the forest, followed by a crowd of crows and magpies and small birds of every sort.

'Here I come!' she shouted in bird-language. For, when Mrs Pepperpot was small she could talk with animals and birds.

A big crow cawed: 'Are you
going to the moon with
that balloon?'

'Not quite, I hope!' said Mrs Pepperpot, and she told them the whole story. The birds all squawked with glee when they heard about the corn and the bird-house she had got for them.

'But first you must help *me*,' said Mrs Pepperpot. 'I want you all to hang onto this balloon string and guide me back to land on my own doorstep.'

So the birds clung to the string with their beaks and claws and, as they flew down to Mrs Pepperpot's house, the balloon looked like a kite with fancy bows tied to its tail.

When Mrs Pepperpot set foot on the ground she instantly grew to her normal size.

So she waved goodbye to the birds
and went indoors to wait for Mr
Pepperpot.

It was late in the evening before Mr Pepperpot came home, tired and miserable after searching everywhere for his lost wife. He put his knapsack down in the hall and carried the sheaf of corn and the bird-house outside. But when he came in again he noticed that the mistletoe had disappeared.

'Oh well,' he said sadly, 'what does it matter now that Mrs Pepperpot is gone?'

He opened the door into the kitchen; there was the mistletoe hanging over the doorway and, under it, as large as life, stood Mrs Pepperpot!

'Darling husband!' she said, as she put her arms round his neck and gave him a great big smacking kiss:

'Happy Christmas!'